Bawdy, McPea's Circus of Fleas

Level 9 – Gold

Helpful Hints for Reading at Home

The focus phonemes (units of sound) used throughout this series are in line with the order in which your child is taught at school. This offers a consistent approach to learning whether reading at home or in the classroom.

HERE ARE SOME COMMON WORDS THAT YOUR CHILD MIGHT FIND TRICKY:

water	where	would	know	thought	through	couldn't
laughed	eyes	once	we're	school	can't	our

TOP TIPS FOR HELPING YOUR CHILD TO READ:

- Encourage your child to read aloud as well as silently to themselves.
- Allow your child time to absorb the text and make comments.
- Ask simple questions about the text to assess understanding.
- Encourage your child to clarify the meaning of new vocabulary.

This book focuses on developing independence, fluency and comprehension. It is a gold level 9 book band.

Bawdy McPea's Circus of Fleas

Written by
Kirsty Holmes

Illustrated by
Rosie Groom

Shawn the flea was too excited to eat.
"Can I eat later, Mum?" asked Shawn. "I want
to go now!"
Shawn was excited because it was his first
night in his new job. He would be working at
his uncle's famous Circus of Fleas!

Shawn had a leaflet all about the circus. The
leaflet had pictures of the stars of the circus.
There were trapeze fleas, strong-fleas, clown
fleas and there was Jigsaw Peach, the Flea
Cannonball! Shawn loved to read about them
and their jaw-dropping feats.

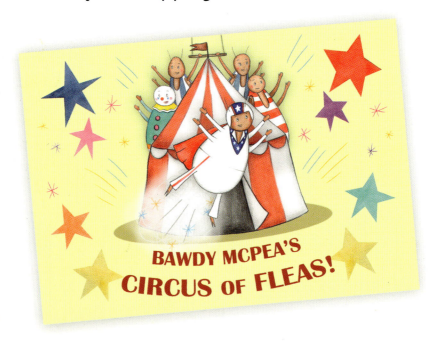

BAWDY MCPEA'S
CIRCUS OF FLEAS!

The bus dropped Shawn off at the gates to the Flea Circus. There was a big sign above the gates. It said:

Bawdy McPea's Circus of Fleas!

There were strange-looking fleas all around. Some wore gleaming costumes. Two large fleas yawned and stretched. It was awesome!

"Excuse me," said Shawn. "Where can I find
Bawdy McPea?"
A huge flea turned to look at Shawn.
"I saw him five minutes ago. He went to get
something to eat," said the flea. "Head to the
Feast Tent. You'll find him there."

Bawdy McPea was a sight to see.
He wore a gleaming top hat, a red coat,
and shiny shoes on his feet. He had a curly
moustache that reached wide across his face.
He beamed when he saw Shawn.

"Shawn! My favourite nephew!" he cried.
"Welcome to my Circus of Fleas!"
"Good to see you, Uncle Bawdy," said Shawn.
"You're looking a bit scrawny!" said Uncle
Bawdy. "Come, join my feast!"
Shawn and Uncle Bawdy sat down to eat.

"So," said Uncle Bawdy, eating a tasty cream cake. "What shall we do with you?"
"I don't know," said Shawn. He took another tasty treat. "I don't think I am good at anything."

"Nonsense!" squeaked Bawdy McPea. "You're a McPea! Every flea who is a McPea is a star! We just have to find your feat."
Shawn and Uncle Bawdy finished their meal.
"Let me show you around my Circus of Fleas!" said Uncle Bawdy.

"First, we shall meet the trapeze fleas," said Uncle Bawdy. "Shawn, meet Heath and Jeanie."
The trapeze fleas had stripy costumes. Shawn was so amazed at their leaps and swoops that his jaw hung open.

"Oh Uncle Bawdy,
please can I try?"
said Shawn.
"That looks
awesome – I want
to fly!"
Heath landed by
Shawn with a thud.

"Are you sure, little Shawn,
that you're ready to leap? If you get it wrong,
we will all end up in a heap!"
"I'm sure," said Shawn.

Shawn crawled out onto the platform. It was
very high. He let out a wavering cry.
"Are you ready?" asked Jeanie. "Remember –
leap, reach, catch. It's easy peasy!"
"I'm OK," said Shawn. Then he took a giant
leap...

Shawn reached out for Heath... but missed! He wobbled and squeaked.

"Oh no," said Bawdy McPea, and covered his eyes.

Shawn, Heath and Jeanie all landed in the net in a heap.

"I'm OK!" said Shawn. "But I don't think I'm a trapeze flea."

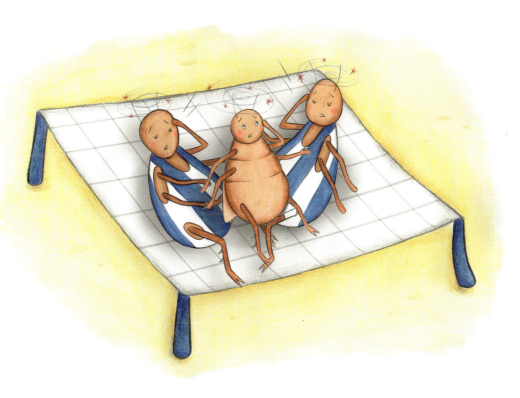

"Next, we will visit the strong-fleas," said Bawdy McPea.

"Hello!" boomed a huge flea. "I'm Squawky. This is The Beast." The two strong-fleas were pushing a huge bean across the circus floor. Squawky the strong-flea reached out to shake Shawn's hand. He was so strong, he lifted Shawn off the ground!

"Oh Uncle Bawdy, can I tag along?" asked Shawn. "That looks so awesome – I want to be strong!"

The Beast put a strong arm on Shawn's shoulder.

"Are you sure, little Shawn, that you're ready to lift? If you get it wrong, we will all end up squished!"

"I'm sure," said Shawn.

Shawn pushed the bean a little. It was very heavy. He let out a little squeal.

"Are you ready?" said Squawky. "You'll need all your brawn to lift this huge bean!"
"I'm OK!" said Shawn. "It will be easy-peasy."
"OK," said The Beast. "One... Two... Three!"
"Heave! Heave!" Shawn yelled. But he weaved and wobbled...
"Oh no," said Bawdy McPea, and covered his eyes.
Shawn, Squawky and The Beast all landed in a heap. They were nearly squished by the bean!
"I'm OK!" said Shawn. "But I don't think I'm a strong-flea."

"I know!" said Bawdy. "Come and see the Little Big Top!"

The clown fleas were sprawling in the sawdust as Shawn and Bawdy sat down. One was making cream pies and another was polishing a seesaw. When he saw Shawn and Bawdy, the biggest clown honked his red nose. "SHOWTIME!"

The clowns leapt and jumped. They fell and caught. They tumbled and rolled. Shawn thought it looked like great fun.

Without even waiting to ask his Uncle Bawdy, Shawn leapt into the ring. He was so excited! He knew this must be his feat!

"Oh, Shawn!" cried Uncle Bawdy. "Be careful!"

Shawn tumbled and rolled. He leapt and jumped. He knew he would be good at it! It had been his dream when he was a little flea to be in the circus one day. He could see it now. Lights, flowers, and an awful lot of clapping and cheering...

"Shawn! Look out!" cried the big clown flea.
But Shawn was still dreaming!
"Oh no," said Bawdy McPea. He covered his eyes.
Shawn rode straight towards a pile of acrobat fleas! And CRASH! They all flew into the table of cream pies.

"Shawn?" said Bawdy. "Are you OK?"
"No," said Shawn.

Shawn went for a walk. He was feeling awful as he weaved between the tents and wagons. "I'm not good at anything," Shawn said. "I'll never find my feat and be a circus flea like Uncle Bawdy."
Suddenly, Shawn heard a splash behind him.

A strange flea wearing a flowery hat and goggles appeared. She gawked down at Shawn from the lip of a thimble.
"Who are you?" asked Shawn.
"Rosa McFlea!" squawked the strange flea. "I read fortunes in this thimble of tea."

"You look awfully glum," said Rosa. "Why do you seem so unhappy?"

"I'm awful at everything," said Shawn. "I just want to find my feat."

"Maybe you are not supposed to find your feat," said Rosa. "Maybe your feat will find you."

"What does that mean?" asked Shawn. Rosa just shrugged, pinched her nose, and took a leap back into the tea.

Shawn stepped backwards and tripped over a rope. He was next to a peach and cream striped tent. A sign said:

JIGSAW PEACH

THE FEARLESS FLEA!

Inside the tent, Shawn could hear shouting.

"What do you mean, Dawn?" yelled Bawdy.

"Why won't he get in the cannon?"

"He's sick and cannot perform his feat!" said a voice.

Shawn looked into the tent. What had happened to Jigsaw Peach?

"Why not?" said Bawdy to Dawn.

"He has eaten too much peach pudding. Oh, this is awful!" cried Dawn.

"The Flea Cannonball is the big finish!" said Bawdy.

"Then we need a new flea," said Dawn. "But where will we find someone like Jigsaw Peach?"

"Good at leaping... Good at crashing... And always OK..." said Bawdy.
"Yes!" cried Dawn. "That's just like Jigsaw Peach. Do you know of such a flea?"
"Dawn, my dear," said Bawdy McPea. "I think the flea we need is..."

"Me!" said Shawn, stepping forwards.
"Indeed," said Bawdy. "Shawn, my dear flea.
I believe we may have found your feat."
"Pleased to meet you, Shawn," said Dawn.
"How do you feel about heights... And loud
noises?"
"I can't wait!" said Shawn.

Dawn helped Shawn get into the suit. It was a
bit awkward. Shawn was much scrawnier than
Jigsaw Peach.
"Don't worry," said Dawn. "We'll stuff it with
sawdust and straw."

"Why do they call him
Jigsaw?" asked Shawn.
"Because they
always have to
put him back
together!"
laughed Dawn.

Everything was ready. Shawn was in the
cannon and Dawn was ready. The lights came
on in the Little Big Top.

"Welcome, friends and fleas, to the Little Big
Top!" cried Bawdy McPea. "We are so pleased
you are having an awesome time here at
Bawdy McPea's Circus of Fleas!"

Ten...
Nine...
Eight...
Seven...
Six...
Five...
"Are you ready?" whispered Dawn.
"I'm ready!" said Shawn.
Dawn lit the match.
"Good luck, Shawn!" she smiled.
Four...
"Good luck, Shawn," said Uncle Bawdy.
Three...
"Fly high, Shawn!" cried Jeanie.
Two...
"Go Shawn! You're awesome, dude!" shouted
Squawky and The Beast.

ONE.

"Go!" shouted Dawn. "See you when you
land!"

Shawn flew higher and higher. As he soared above the crowd, his suit gleamed. His smile widened. He felt like a streak of sparkles and colour, flying over the crowds below.

He looked down and saw his mum and dad.
They were leaning on each other and smiling
too. Shawn had found his feat!
And he felt awesome.

Bawdy, McPea's Circus of Fleas

1. Why was Shawn too excited to eat?

2. Where did the bus drop Shawn off?

3. What were the strong–fleas called?

4. What was Rosa McFlea wearing?

    (a) A red scarf and goggles

    (b) A flowery hat and goggles

    (c) A spotty top and hat

5. How did Shawn feel when he shot out of the cannon? Have you ever felt like this?

©2020 **BookLife Publishing Ltd.**
King's Lynn, Norfolk PE30 4LS

ISBN 978-1-83927-013-0

Bawdy McPea's Circus of Fleas
Written by Kirsty Holmes
Illustrated by Rosie Groom

An Introduction to BookLife Readers...

Our Readers have been specifically created in line with the London Institute of Education's approach to book banding and are phonetically decodable and ordered to support each phase of the Letters and Sounds document.

Each book has been created to provide the best possible reading and learning experience. Our aim is to share our love of books with children, providing both emerging readers and prolific page-turners with beautiful books that are guaranteed to provoke interest and learning, regardless of ability.

BOOK BAND GRADED using the Institute of Education's approach to levelling.

PHONETICALLY DECODABLE supporting each phase of Letters and Sounds.

EXERCISES AND QUESTIONS to offer reinforcement and to ascertain comprehension.

BEAUTIFULLY ILLUSTRATED to inspire and provoke engagement, providing a variety of styles for the reader to enjoy whilst reading through the series.

AUTHOR INSIGHT:
KIRSTY HOLMES

Kirsty Holmes, holder of a BA, PGCE, and an MA, was born in Norfolk, England. She has written over 60 books for BookLife Publishing, and her stories are full of imagination, creativity and fun.

This book focuses on developing independence, fluency and comprehension. It is a gold level 9 book band.